Easy
DINOSAUR
Mazes

PATRICIA J. WYNNE

DOVER PUBLICATIONS, INC.
Mineola, New York

Note

In this exciting maze book, you will help a baby *Triceratops* (try-**serr**-uh-**tops**) escape from a large dinosaur, show a thirsty *Dryosaurus* (**dry**-oh-**sore**-us) how to get safely to water, and find the path for a *Baryonyx* (**bare**-ee-**on**-ix) to take to catch a big fish.

We have learned about dinosaurs from studying their bones and teeth, which tell us what dinosaurs looked like and what they ate. Some dinosaurs, like the *Lambeosaurus* (**lam**-bee-oh-**sore**-us), ate plants. Others were meat eaters, like the *Deinonychus* (dye-**non**-ih-kuss). Some ate both plants and meat, such as the *Gallimimus* (**gal**-uh-**my**-muss). After each dinosaur name, you will find the right way to say it.

For each of the 37 puzzles, you will look for the right way to get through the maze. Using a pencil, draw a line from the START to the FINISH and show the path to take. If you need help, you can turn to the Solutions section, which begins on page 39 (but try your hardest first). When you have finished all of the mazes, you can have even more fun by coloring in the pages with crayons or colored pencils. Let's get started—the dinosaurs are waiting!

Bibliographical Note

Easy Dinosaur Mazes is a new work, first published by Dover Publications, Inc., in 2007.

International Standard Book Number: 0-486-45363-4

Manufactured in the United States of America
Dover Publications, Inc., 31 East 2nd Street, Mineola, N.Y. 11501

START

FINISH

The *Mosasaurus* (**mose**-uh-**sore**-us) lives in the sea. Help this dinosaur find her way to the fish that she will have for lunch.

START

FINISH

These *Apatosaurs* (uh-**pat**-uh-**sores**) are leaving for a new home.
Help the young one at the top find his way to the group.

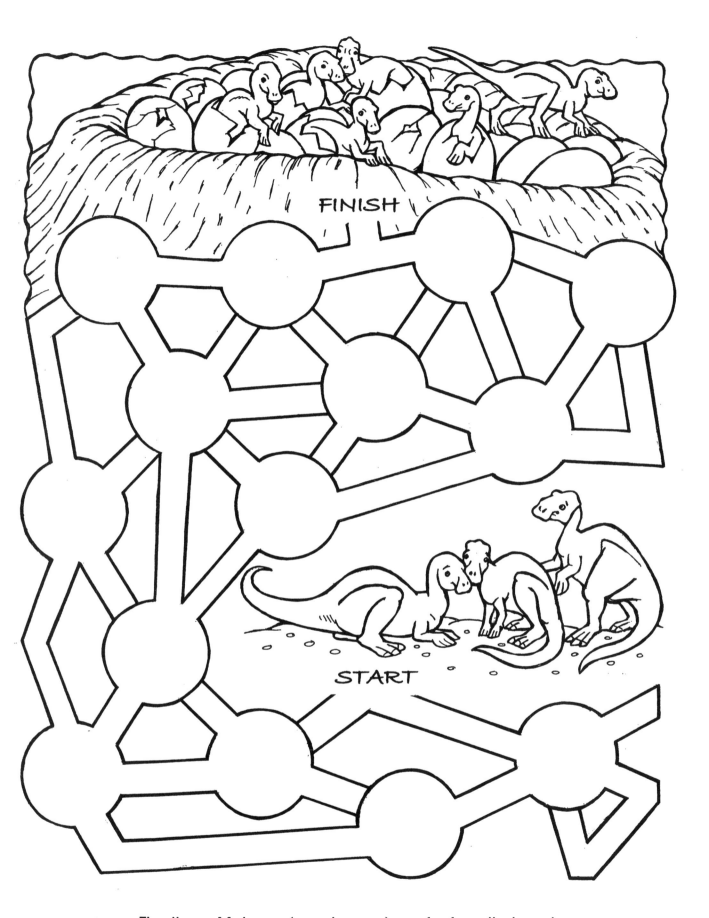

The three *Maisaurs* (**my**-uh-**sores**) are far from their nest.
Show them the way to get back to it.

START

FINISH

Look out for the *Carnosaur* (**car**-no-**sore**). He has big teeth!
Can you find the way to get around him and escape?

4

The little animal at the top wants to get down from the spiny
Styracosaurus (sty-**rack**-uh-**sore**-us). Please show her the way.

FINISH

START

There's only one plant left for this *Dacentrurus* (dah-sen-**true**-russ) to eat.
Show him how to get to it.

START

FINISH

Do you see the *Longisquama* (lawn-jiss-**kwam**-uh) at the top? Help him find the way through the group of long-necked *Tanystropheus* (**tan**-ee-**stro**-fee-us).

The *Baryonyx* (**bare**-ee-**on**-ix) eats fish. She would like to catch the big one at the bottom. Show this dinosaur the way to her food.

Help the *Ammonite* (**am**-uh-night) at the top left sneak past the long-necked *Elasmosaurus* (eh-**lazz**-muh-**sore**-us) to find the other Ammonites. The Elasmosaurus was not a dinosaur—it was an enormous sea creature.

Help the bee at the top buzz past the sharp-clawed *Troödon* (**tro**-oh-don) to safely reach the flowers at the bottom.

START

FINISH

The large-jawed *Criorhynchus* (cry-oh-**ring**-kuss) was a flying reptile.
Show the sea bird the path to take to get to the birds at the bottom.

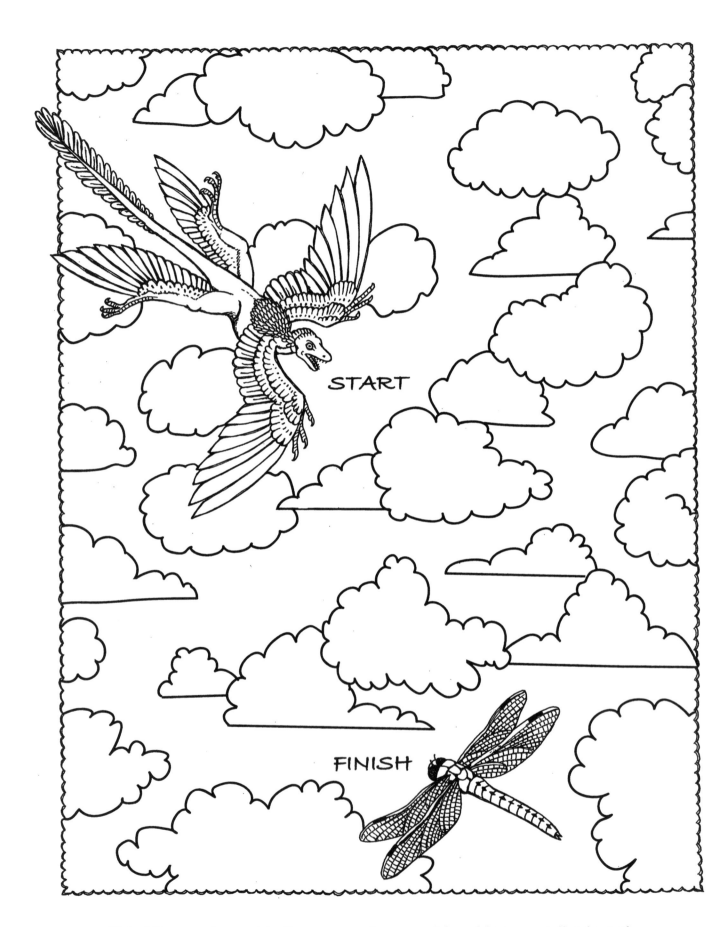

START

FINISH

This *Microraptor gui* (**mike**-row-**rap**-tor guay) has his eye on the insect at the bottom. Show this flying dinosaur how to get to the insect.

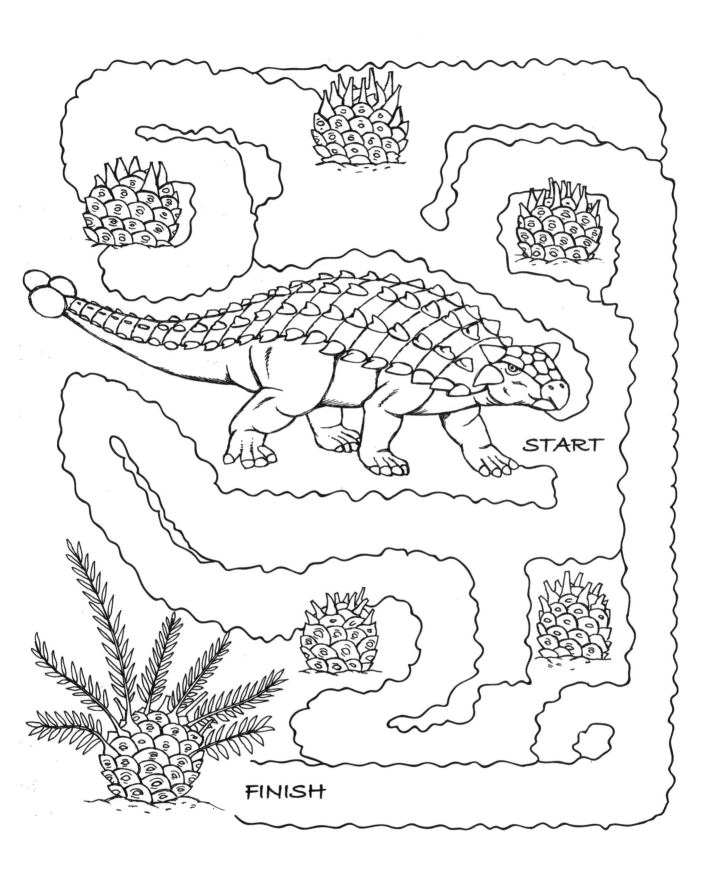

START

FINISH

Nearly all of the plants have been eaten! Help the *Ankylosaurus*
(**ann**-kih-lo-**sore**-us) get to the plant at the end so she can eat.

13

FINISH

START

The large dinosaur at the bottom is getting close to the baby *Triceratops* (try-**serr**-uh-tops).
Help the baby escape to the end of the path, where he will be safe.

14

START

FINISH

This *Brachiosaurus* (**brack**-ee-oh-**sore**-us) needs to reach the leaves at the top.
Help him find the way to the end of the path.

15

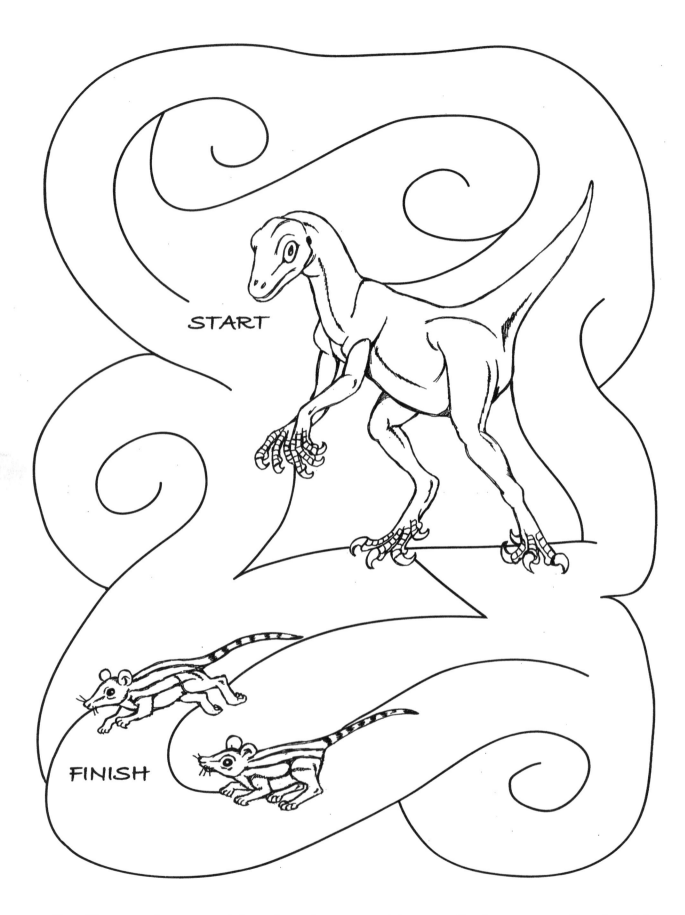

START

FINISH

The *Stenonychosaurus* (sten-uh-**ny**-ko-**sore**-us) has spotted some small animals!
Show this dinosaur the way to go to reach the animals.

This group of small dinosaurs wants to reach the leaves at the top.
Please help them find the way to get there.

START

FINISH

The *marine crocodile* is chasing the fish at the bottom. Help the
crocodile find the way through the water to reach the fish.

18

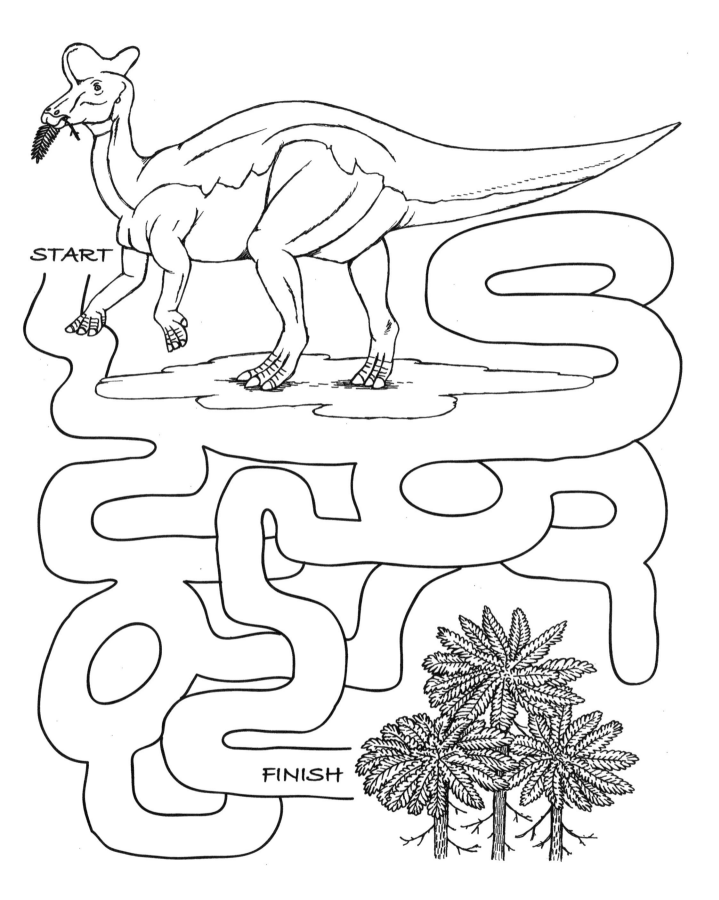

START

FINISH

The *Lambeosaurus* (**lam**-bee-oh-**sore**-us) would like to eat some more of those tasty leaves on the trees at the bottom. Show him the way to get to them.

19

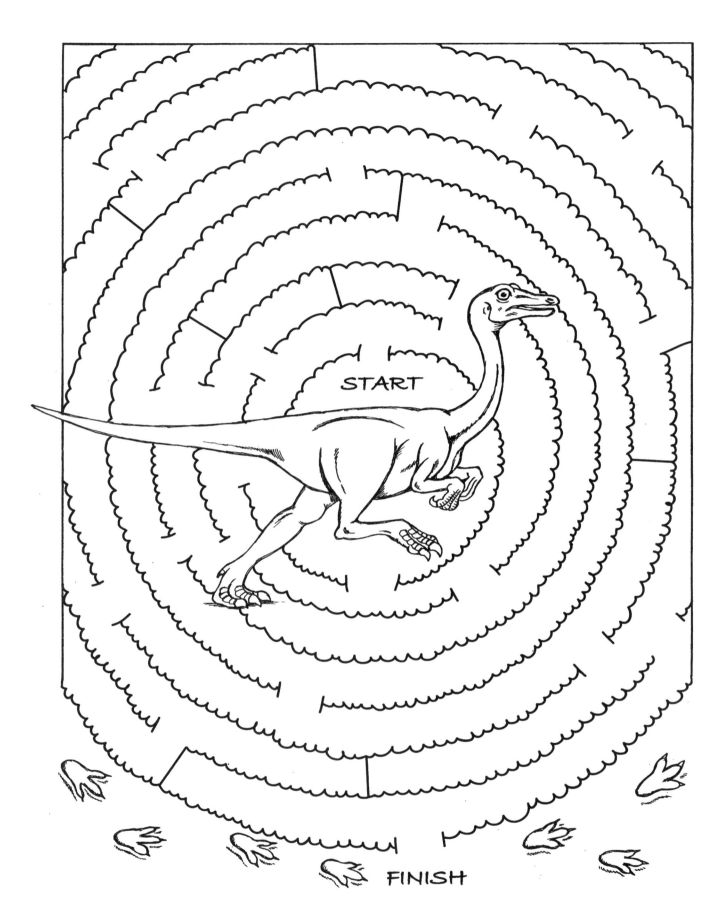

START

FINISH

This *Gallimimus* (**gal**-uh-**my**-muss) has lost her way.
Show her the path to take to get to the footprints.

START

FINISH

The large *Oviraptor* (**oh**-vih-**rap**-tore) is busy guarding her eggs. Help the small Oviraptor get to the end of the path to chase away the creature at the bottom.

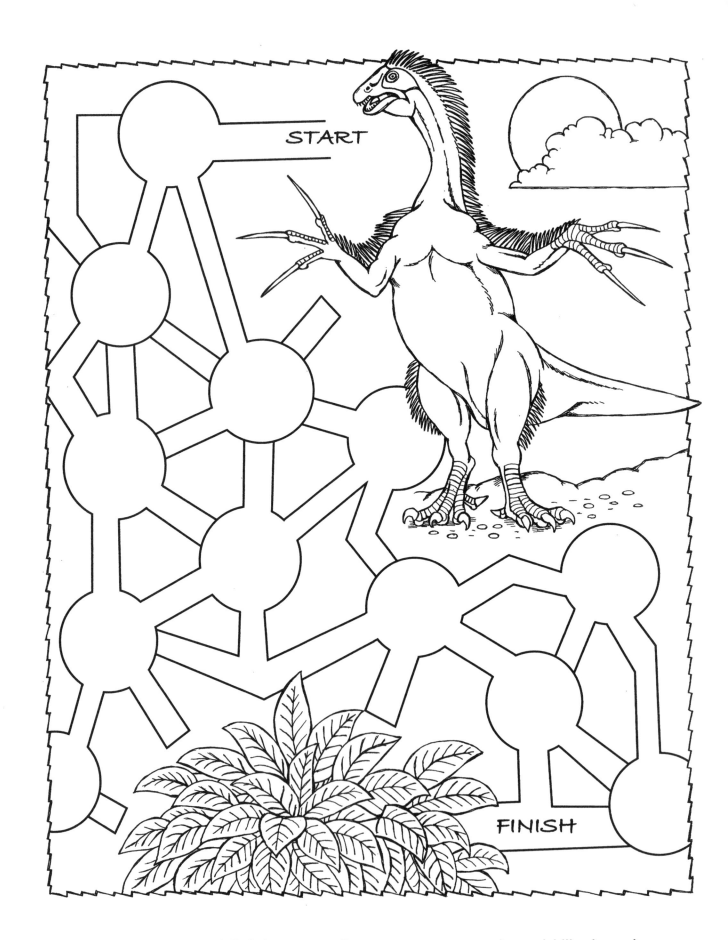

START

FINISH

A long-clawed *Beipiaosaurus* (bay-pea-you-**sore**-us) would like to get to the leafy plant at the bottom. Won't you guide him to the plant?

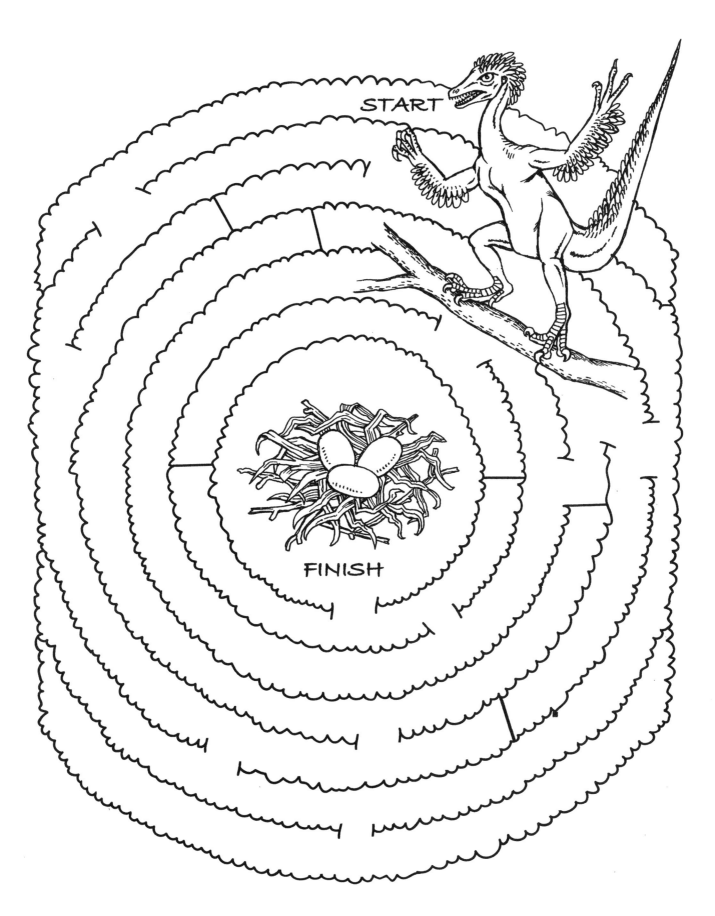

START

FINISH

The feathered *Sinornithosaurus* (**sigh**-nor-nith-oh-**sore**-us) needs to get to the nest in the middle of the path. Find the best way to get there.

START

FINISH

The little *Deinonychus* (dye-**non**-ih-kuss) at the top wants to cross
the river to get to his friends. Please show him the path to take.

START

FINISH

This fierce-looking *Plateosaurus* (**platt**-ee-oh-**sore**-us) is hungry.
Show her how to get to the plants at the bottom.

START

FINISH

Protoceratops (**pro**-toe-**serr**-uh-tops) eggs were some of the first dinosaur eggs ever found. The Protoceratops at the top needs to get to her babies at the bottom—please show the way!

START

FINISH

The *Icthyosaurus* (**ick**-thee-oh-**sore**-us) is shaped like a fish. This Icthyosaurus is trying to get to the sea turtle. Can you find the right path for him to take?

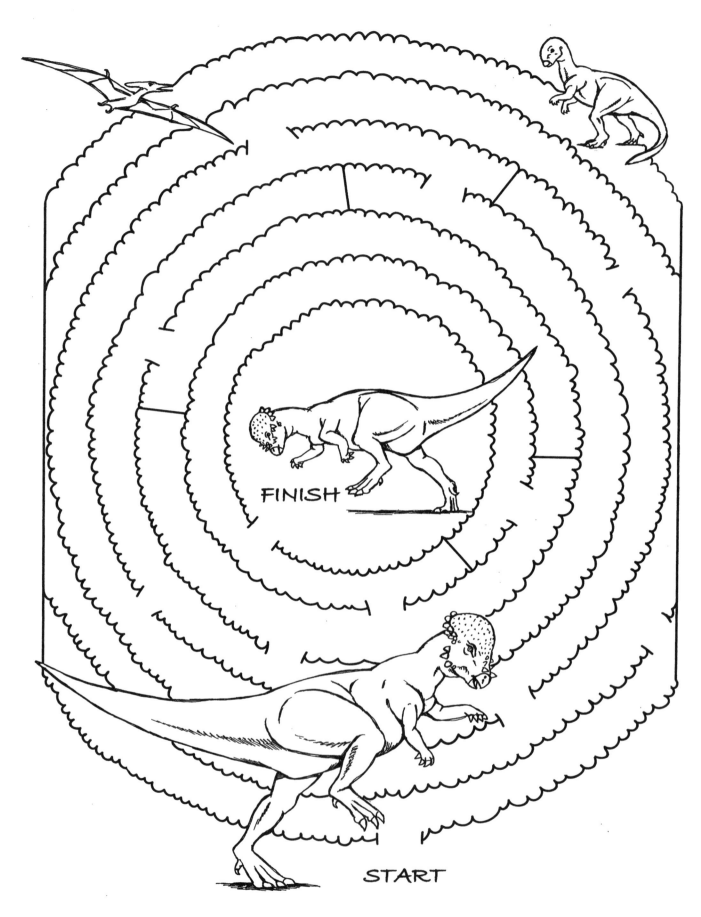

FINISH

START

The thick-skulled *Pachycephalosaurus* (pack-ih-**seff**-uh-low-**sore**-us) at the bottom wants to reach the dinosaur in the middle of the path. Show him the way.

28

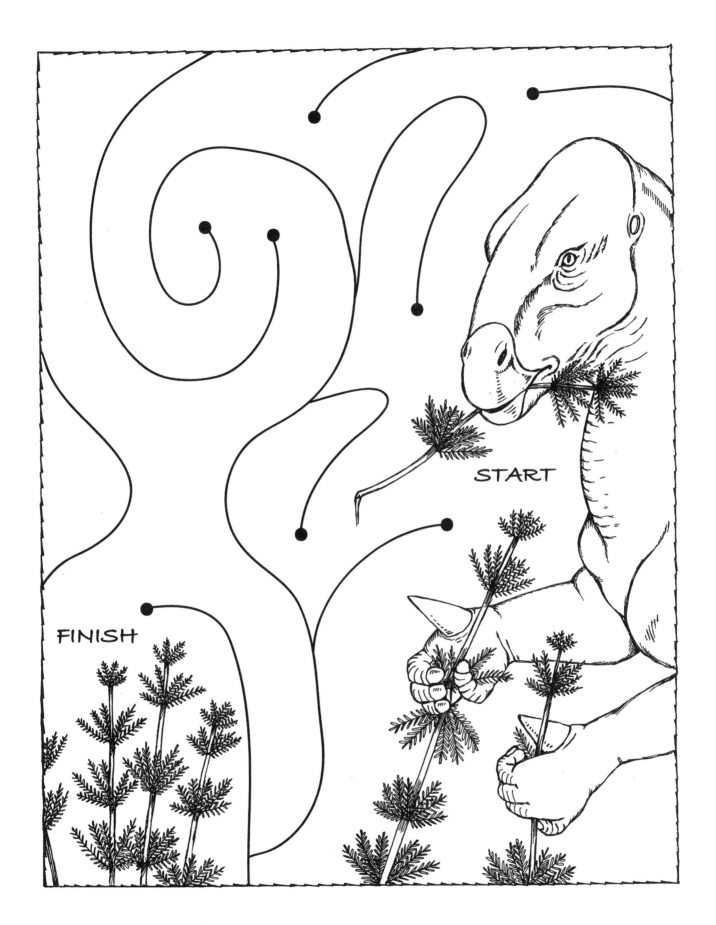

START

FINISH

This *Iguanadon* (ih-**gwon**-uh-don) is munching on some horsetail plants and sees more at the end of the path. Find the way for her to get to them.

Some people think that the *Parasaurolophus* (par-uh-**sore**-oh-**loaf**-us) used the long part of its head to make sounds. Help this Parasaurolophus find the way to the dinosaur at the top.

START

FINISH

The *Quetzalcoatlus* (**kett**-sull-ko-**ott**-luss) was the biggest animal ever to fly.
Show this flying dinosaur the way to get to its meal at the end of the path.

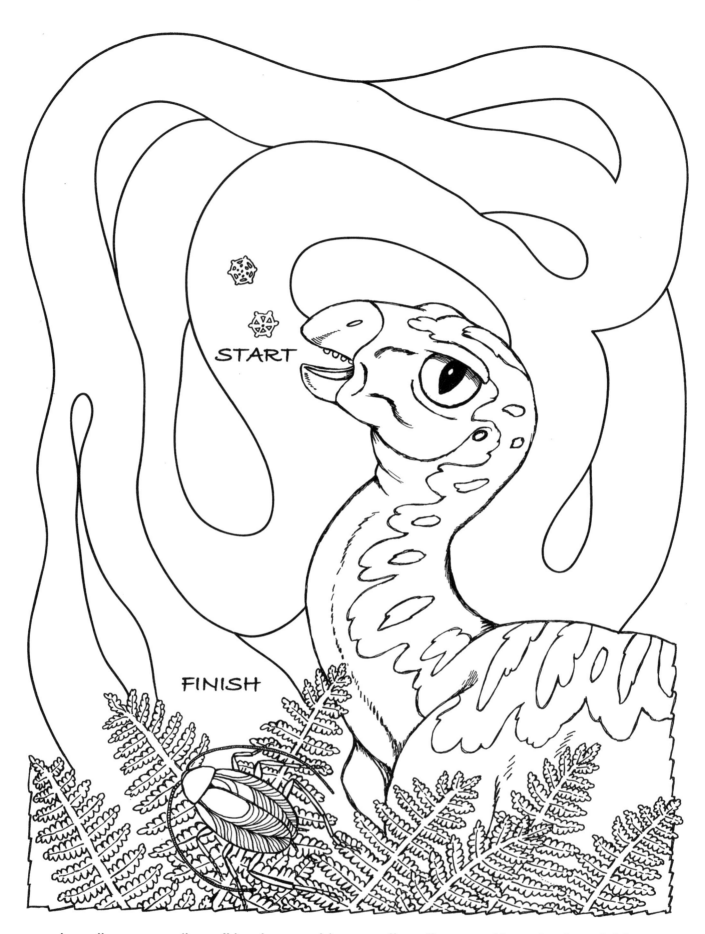

Leaellynosaura (lee-**ell**-in-uh-**sore**-uh) was a tiny dinosaur. Here she is catching snowflakes. Please help her find the way to the insect at the end of the path.

32

START

FINISH

Some dinosaurs swallowed rocks to help grind their food. This young *Stegosaurus* (**steg**-oh-**sore**-us) needs to get to the little rocks in the middle—please show her the way.

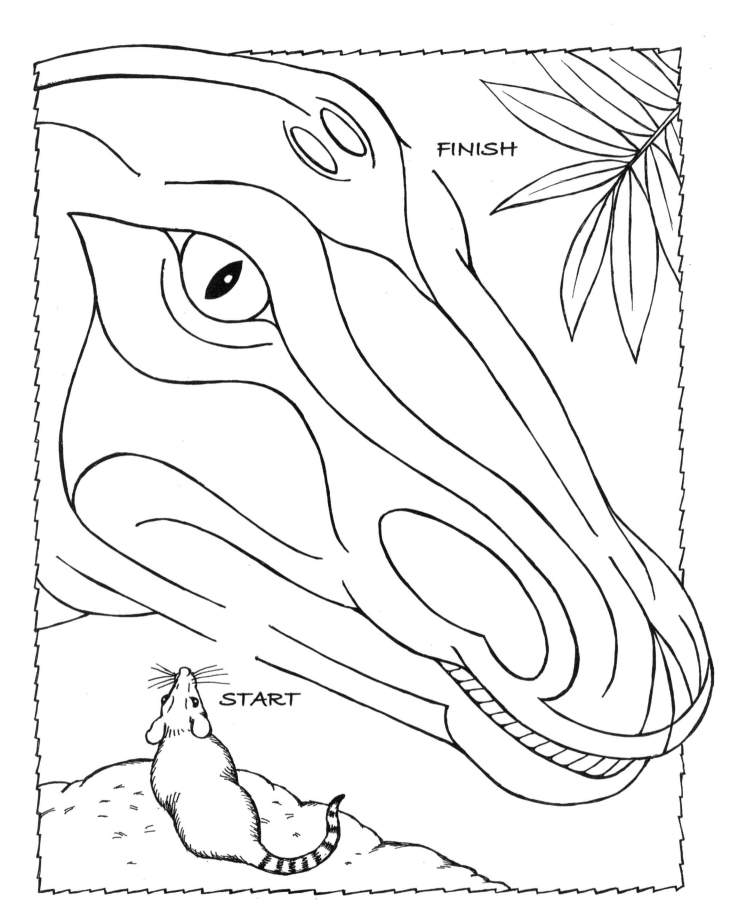

FINISH

START

Alamosaurus (al-uh-moe-**sore**-us) was one of the last of the giant dinosaurs. Help the little animal along the path on the Alamosaurus to the leaf on the other side.

34

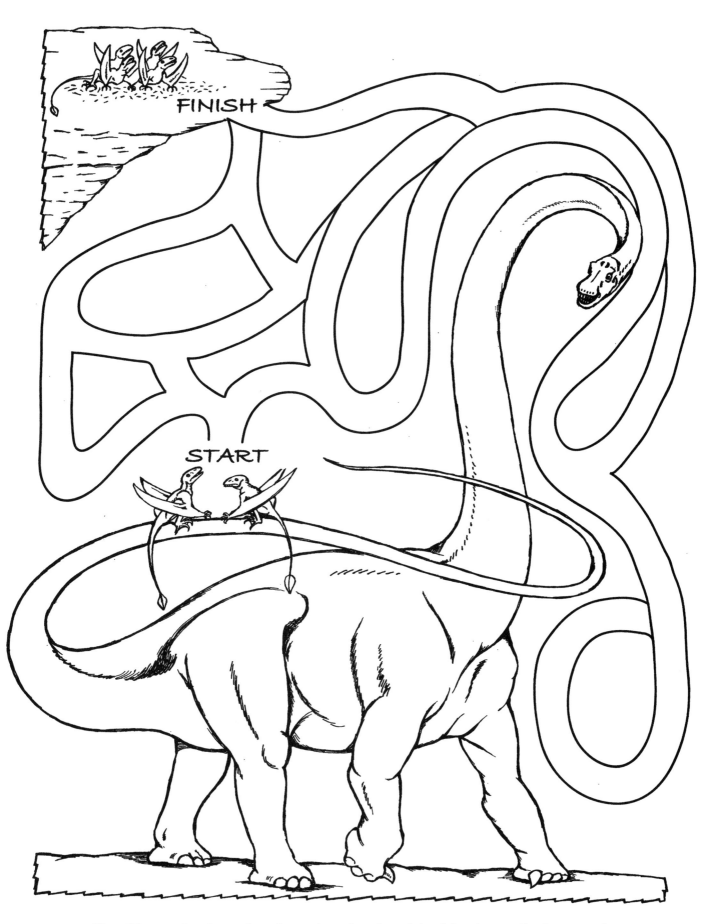

The *Rhamphorhynchus* (ram-foe-**ring**-kuss) babies hope their parents
can find their way home past the *Diplodocus* (dih-**plod**-oh-kuss)!

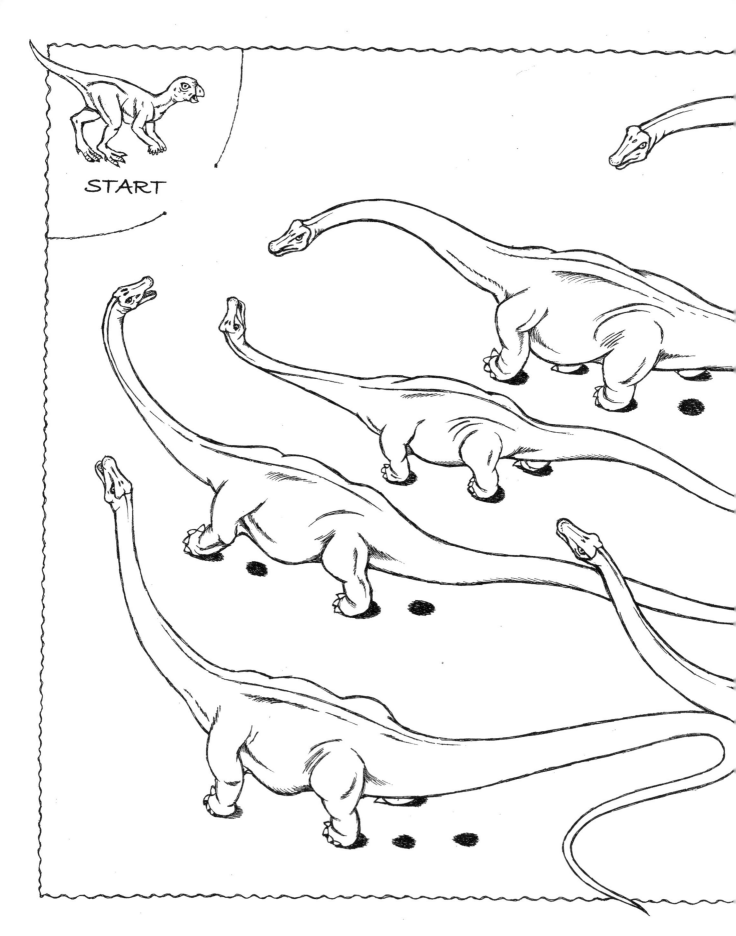

START

The small *Dryosaurus* (**dry**-oh-**sore**-us) at the top is thirsty. Help it get to the stream beyond the group of *Diplodocus* (dih-**plod**-oh-kuss).

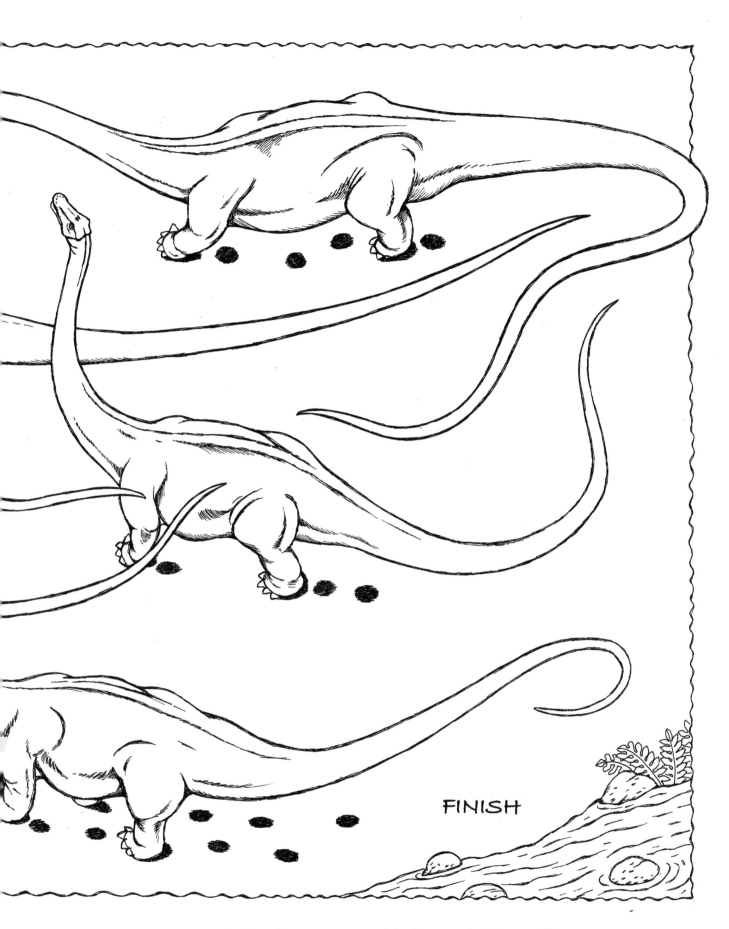

FINISH

Please help the *Dryosaurus* get to the end of the path so
that it can drink from the stream.

START

FINISH

The *Dilophosaurus* (dye-**loff**-oh-**sore**-us) needs to get to the skeleton at the end of the path. Find the way for it to get past the *Shunosaurus* (**shoe**-no-**sore**-us) and its dangerous tail.

Solutions

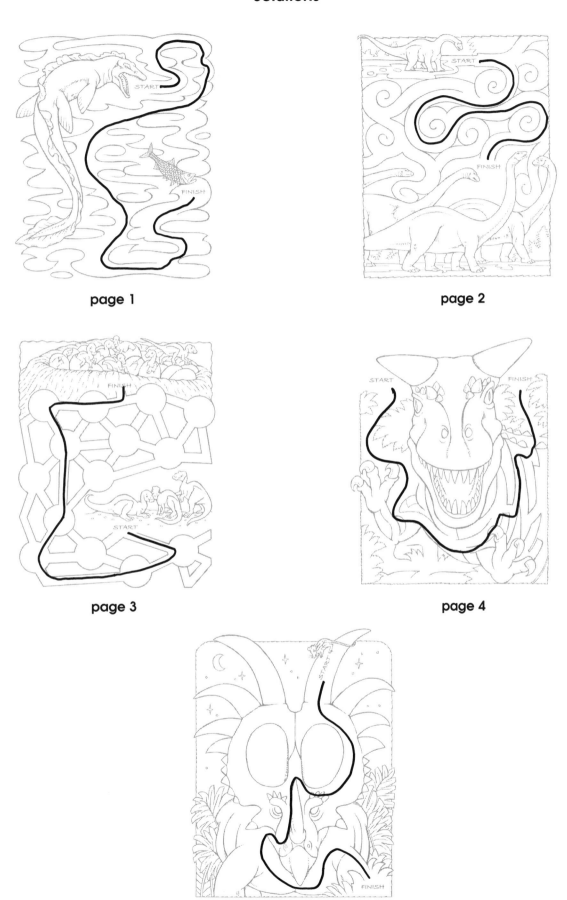

page 1

page 2

page 3

page 4

page 5

page 6

page 7

page 8

page 9

page 10

40

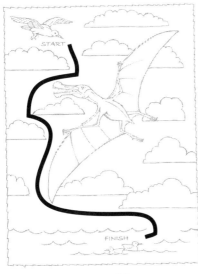

page 11

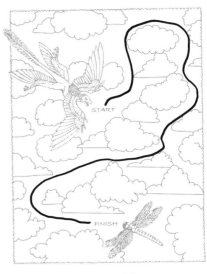

page 12

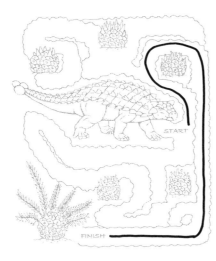

page 13

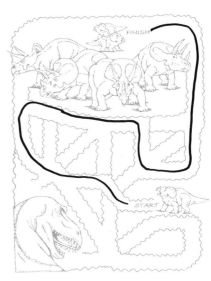

page 14

page 15

page 16

page 17

page 18

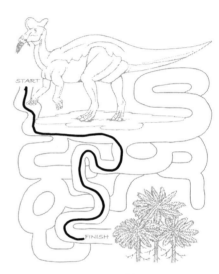
page 19

page 20

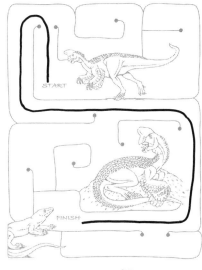

page 21

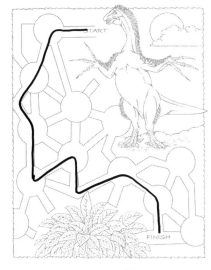

page 22

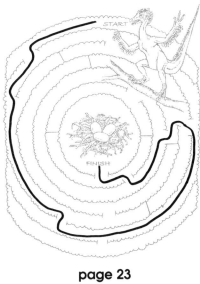

page 23

page 24

page 25

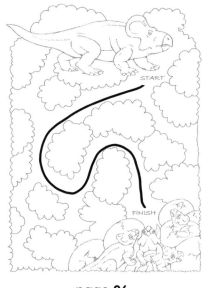

page 26

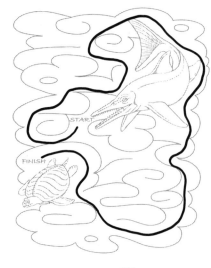

page 27

page 28

page 29

page 30

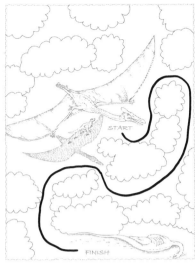

page 31

page 32

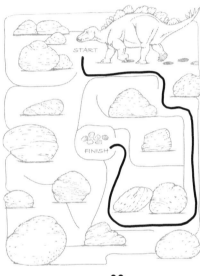

page 33

page 34

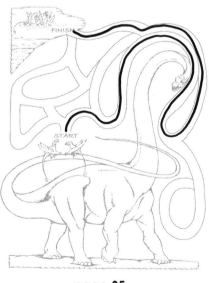

page 35

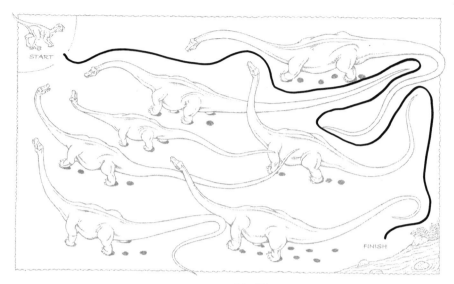

pages 36-37

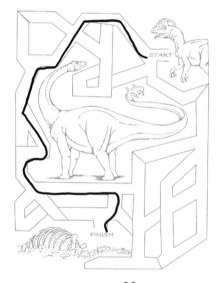

page 38